Burp, Hip, and Twist

A Journey Into the Caves

Bruce Charles Kirrage

Ordering Information:

For orders and inquiries, please contact:
1-888-404-1388
www.goldtouchpress.com
book.orders@goldtouchpress.com

Printed in the United States of America

The three Littluns - Burp, Hip, and Twist had gone into the woods one day to see what they could see.

Hip carried a flask of tea,
Burp had some sandwiches and Twist,
of course, had his MP3 player on,
very loud to scare away any ghosts
that may be lurking because
it was getting dark.

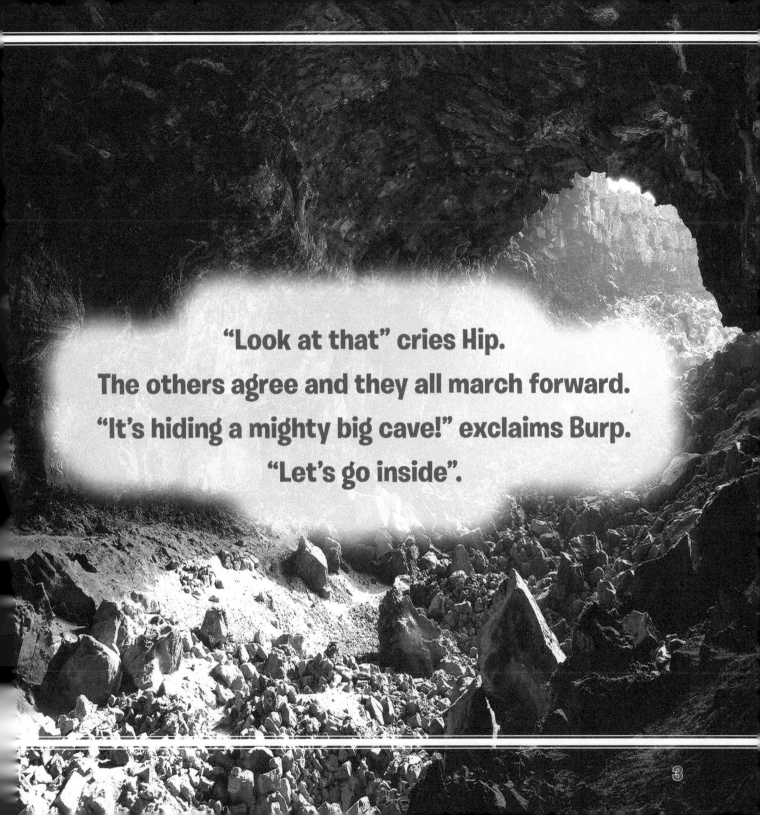

"Look at that" cries Hip.

The others agree and they all march forward.

"It's hiding a mighty big cave!" exclaims Burp.

"Let's go inside".

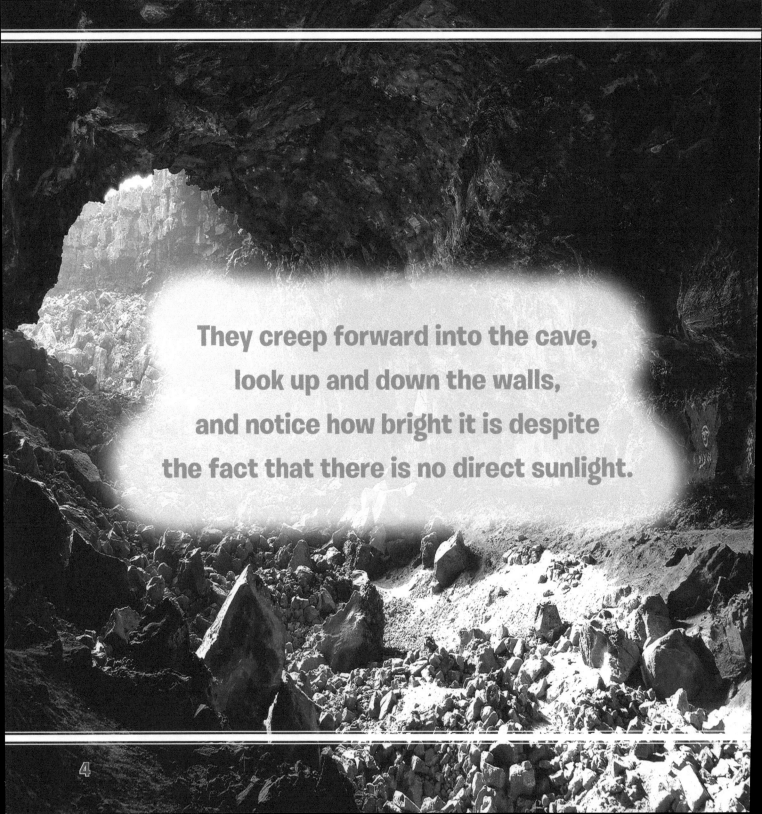

They creep forward into the cave,
look up and down the walls,
and notice how bright it is despite
the fact that there is no direct sunlight.

"I know what that is" says Twist.
"It's Phosphur".
"Phosphur?"
ask the others very puzzled.

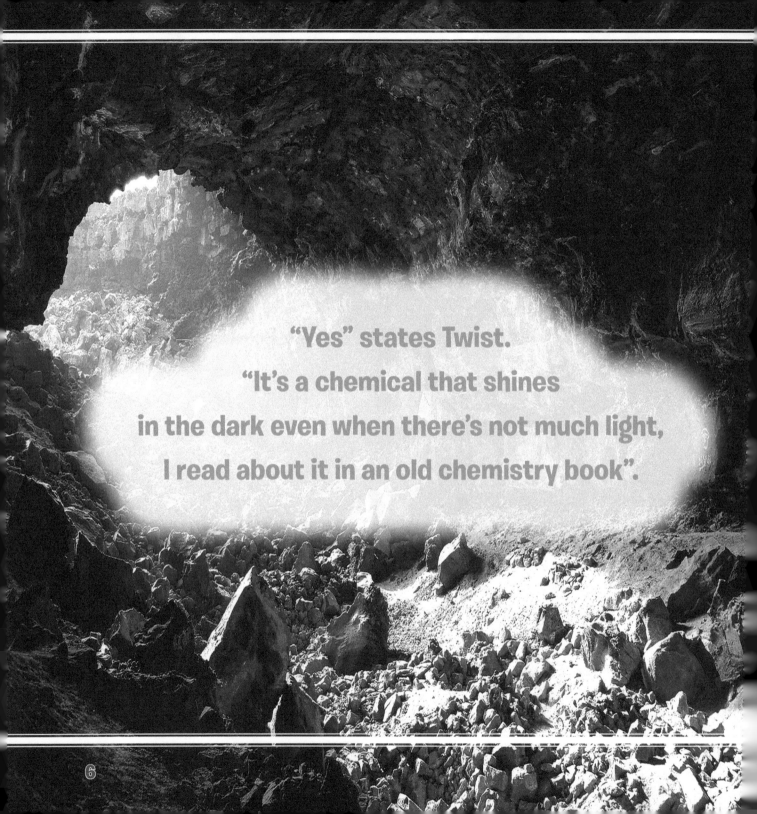

"Yes" states Twist.
"It's a chemical that shines
in the dark even when there's not much light,
I read about it in an old chemistry book".

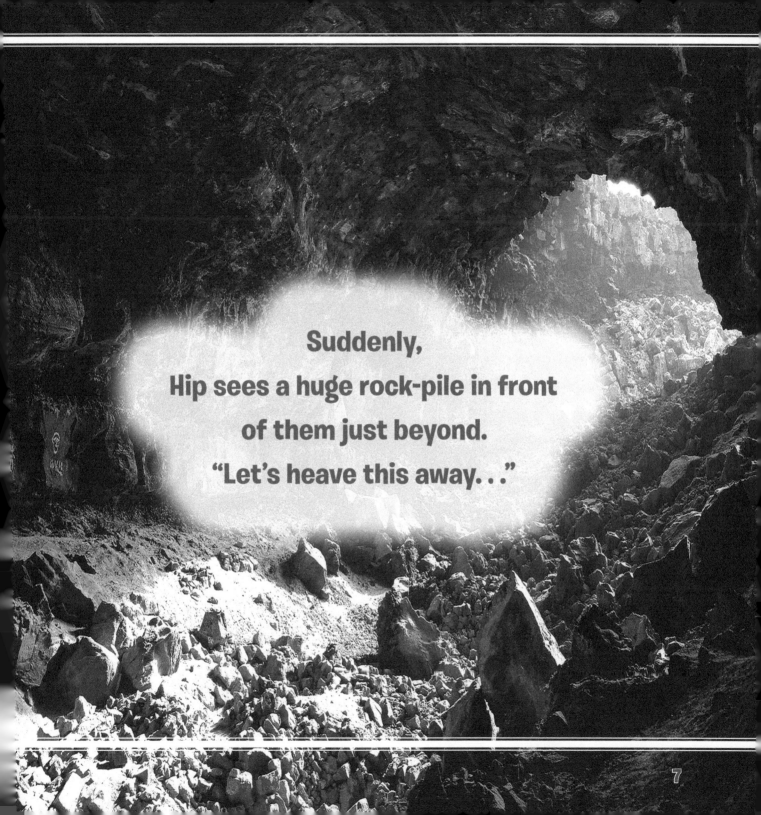

Suddenly,
Hip sees a huge rock-pile in front
of them just beyond.
"Let's heave this away..."

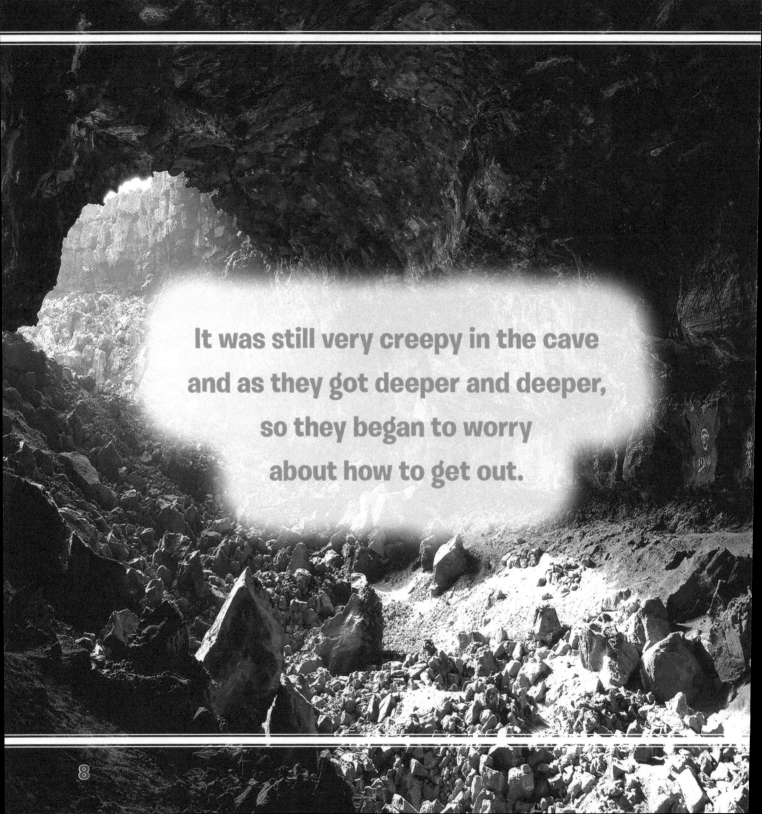

It was still very creepy in the cave
and as they got deeper and deeper,
so they began to worry
about how to get out.

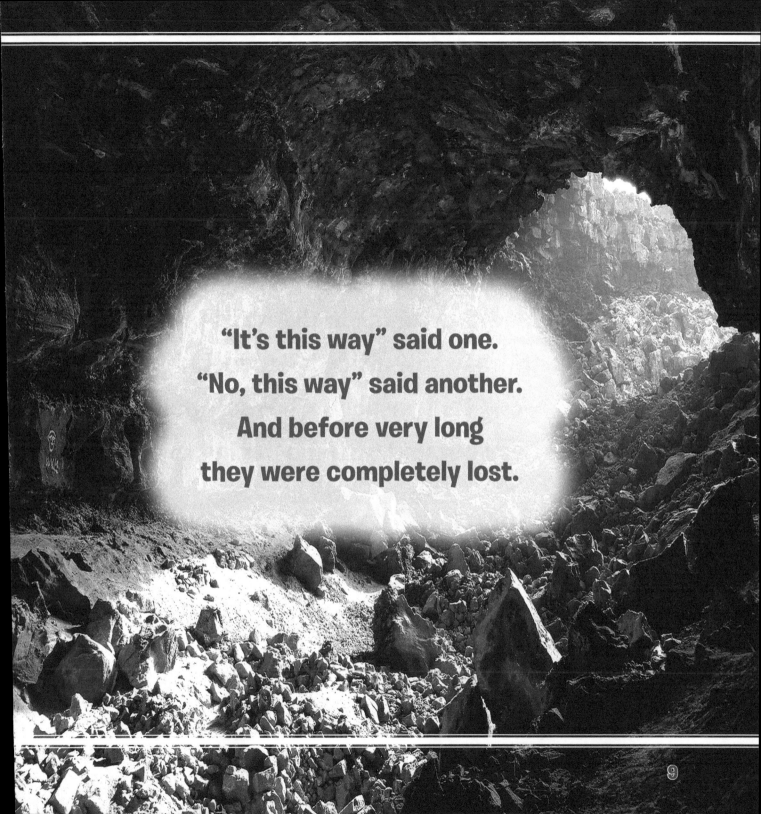

"It's this way" said one.
"No, this way" said another.
And before very long
they were completely lost.

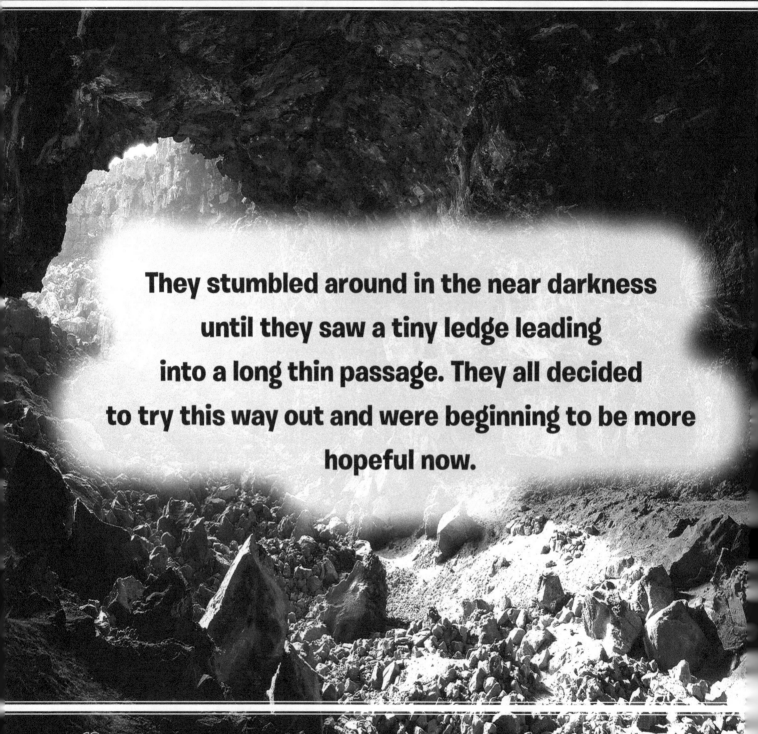

They stumbled around in the near darkness
until they saw a tiny ledge leading
into a long thin passage. They all decided
to try this way out and were beginning to be more
hopeful now.

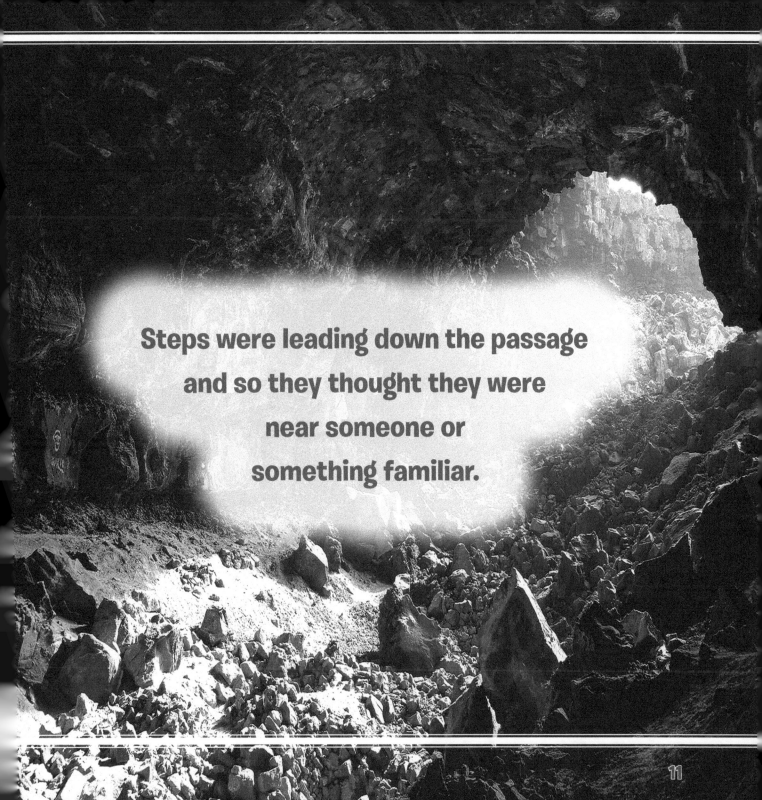

Steps were leading down the passage and so they thought they were near someone or something familiar.

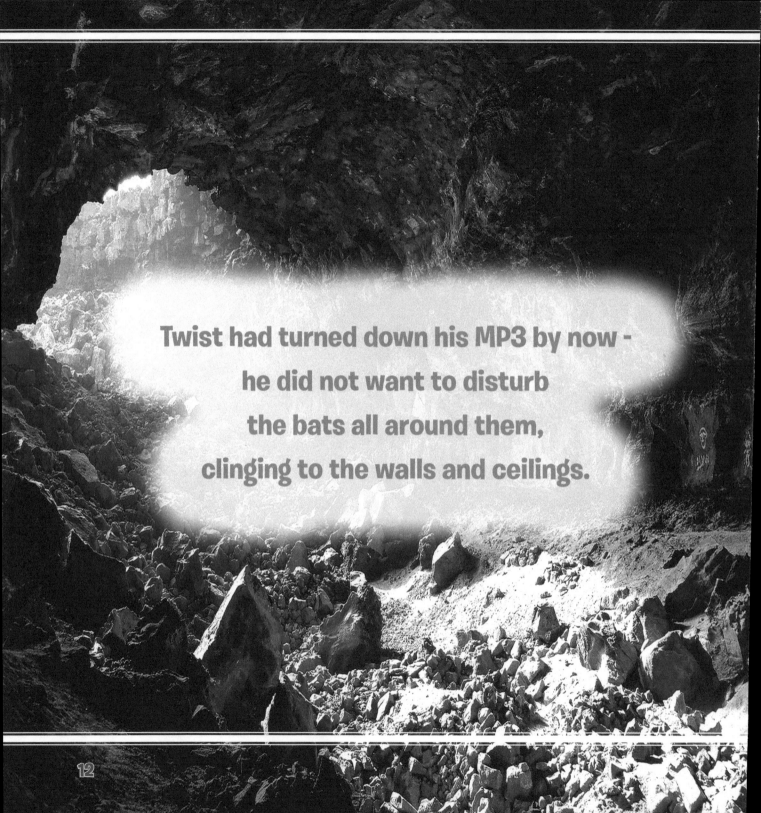

Twist had turned down his MP3 by now -
he did not want to disturb
the bats all around them,
clinging to the walls and ceilings.

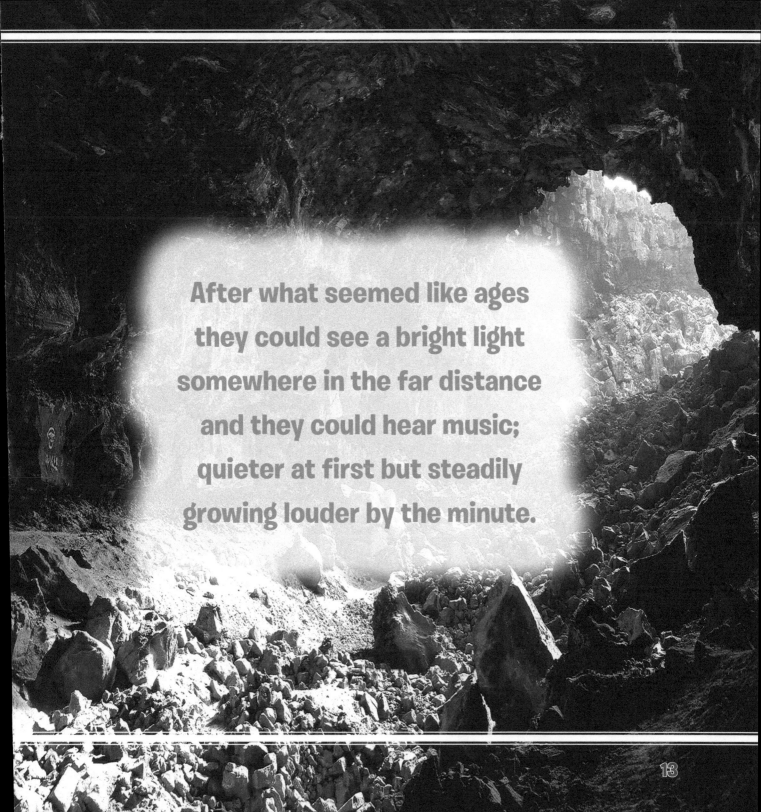

After what seemed like ages they could see a bright light somewhere in the far distance and they could hear music; quieter at first but steadily growing louder by the minute.

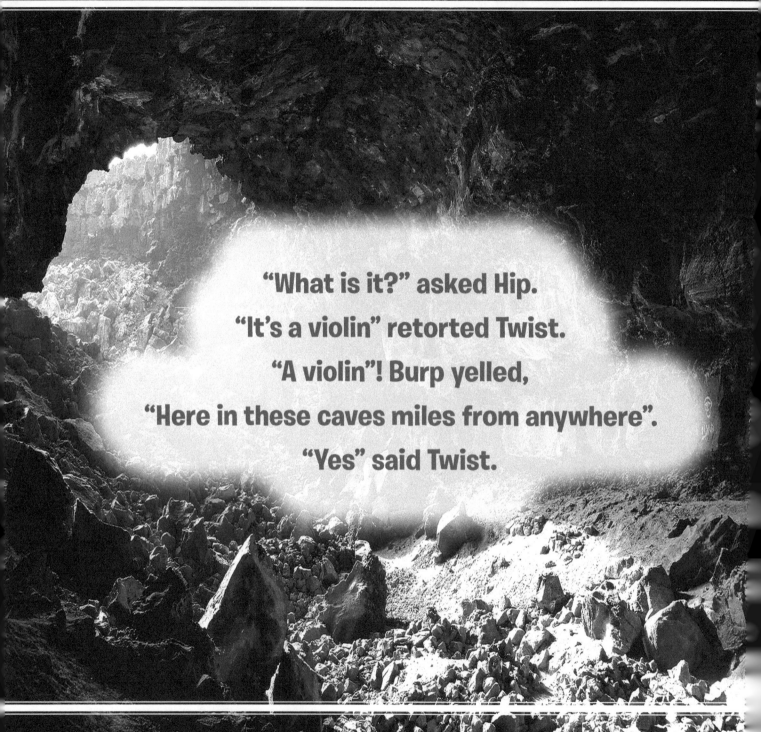

"What is it?" asked Hip.

"It's a violin" retorted Twist.

"A violin"! Burp yelled,

"Here in these caves miles from anywhere".

"Yes" said Twist.

By now the music was quite loud and suddenly they all popped out into a large room, full of people. They were sitting down watching a girl and a boy being rowed across an underground lake on a Gondola with a man playing a violin to them. The orchestra who were on another craft; and the people in the audience held their breath waiting for the man to finish playing his tune.

And they could not believe their eyes and ears.
Twist decided to record all of it on
his MP3 player.

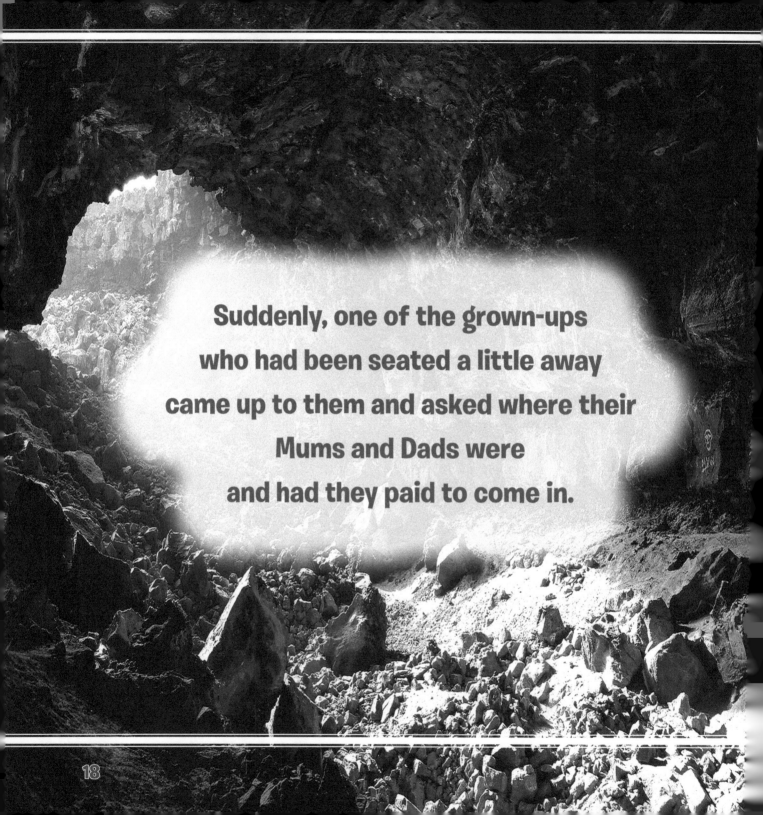

Suddenly, one of the grown-ups
who had been seated a little away
came up to them and asked where their
Mums and Dads were
and had they paid to come in.

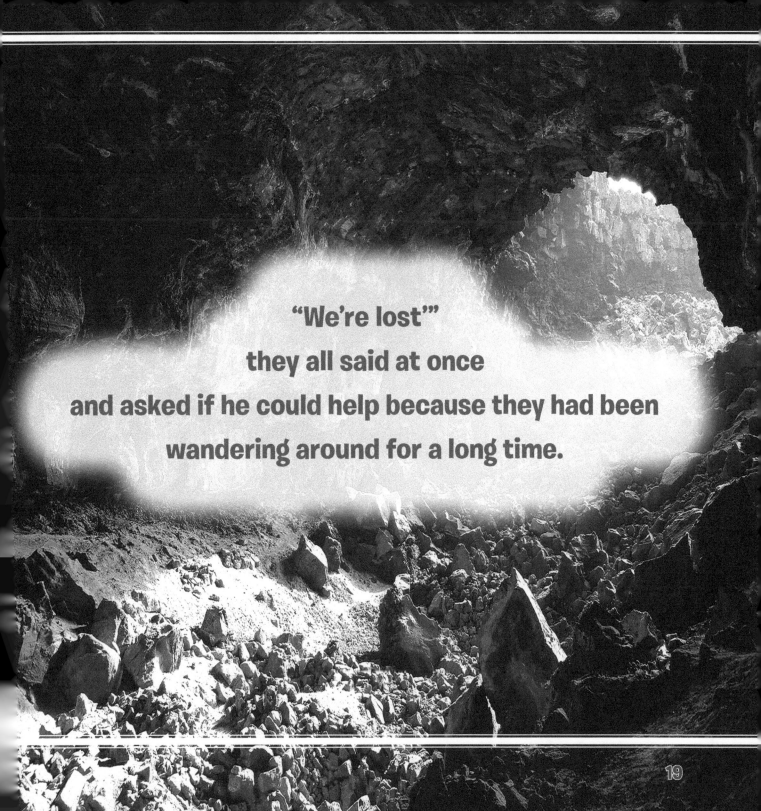

"We're lost"
they all said at once
and asked if he could help because they had been
wandering around for a long time.

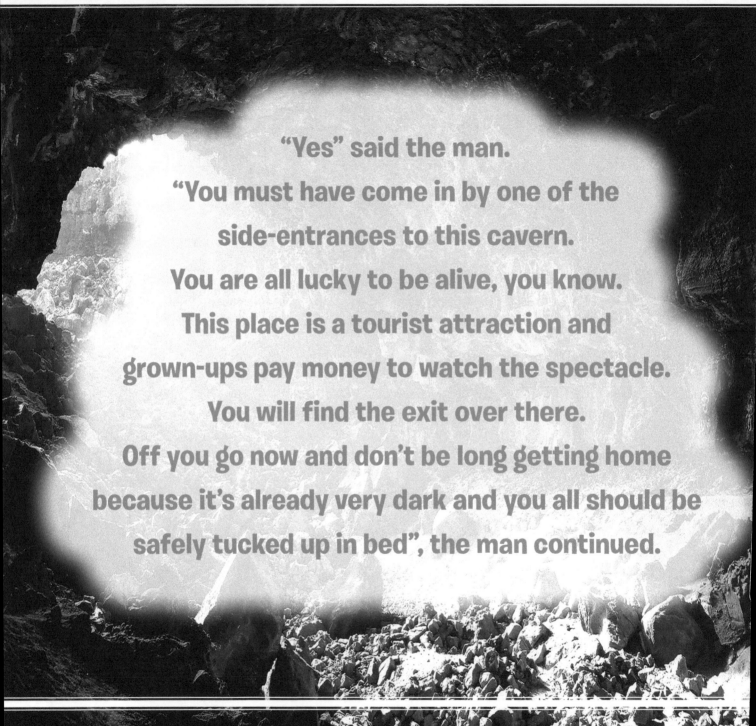

"Yes" said the man.

"You must have come in by one of the side-entrances to this cavern.

You are all lucky to be alive, you know.

This place is a tourist attraction and grown-ups pay money to watch the spectacle.

You will find the exit over there.

Off you go now and don't be long getting home because it's already very dark and you all should be safely tucked up in bed", the man continued.

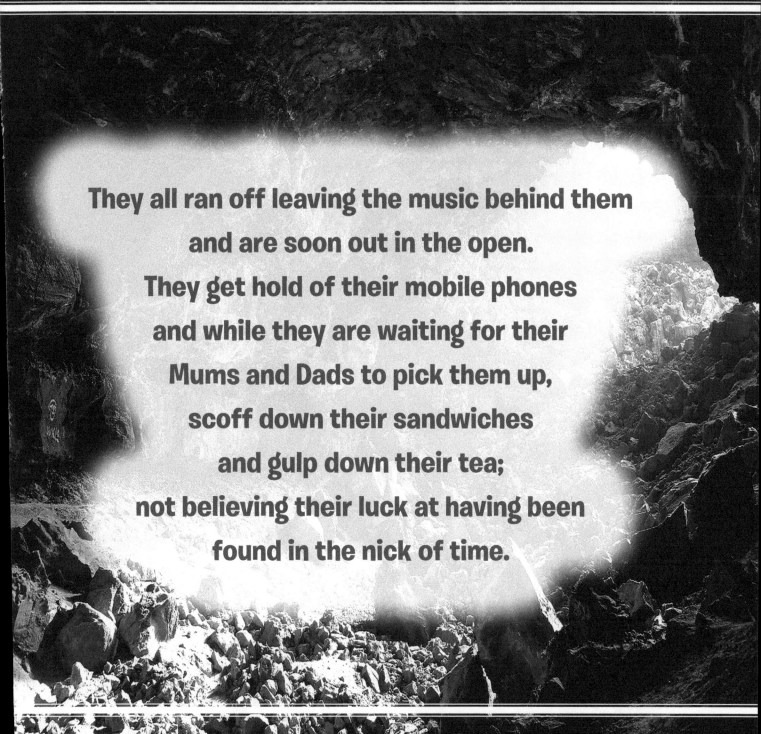

They all ran off leaving the music behind them
and are soon out in the open.
They get hold of their mobile phones
and while they are waiting for their
Mums and Dads to pick them up,
scoff down their sandwiches
and gulp down their tea;
not believing their luck at having been
found in the nick of time.

CPSIA information can be obtained
at www.ICGtesting.com
Printed in the USA
BVHW012302071222
653747BV00005B/25